The Midnight Gang

Written by **Margaret Wild**

Illustrated by **Ann James**

SOUTHWOOD
B O O K S

For John and Leonore
M.W.

Daniel

For sweet baby James
∧ A.J.

Ann James used chalk pastels on coloured papers
for the illustrations in this book.

Southwood Books Limited,
4 Southwood Lawn Road,
London N6 5SF

First published in Australia by Omnibus Books 1996

This edition published in the UK under licence from Omnibus Books by
Southwood Books Limited, 2000.

Text copyright © Margaret Wild 1996
Illustrations copyright © Ann James 1996

ISBN 1-903207-05-3

Printed in Hong Kong

A CIP catalogue record for this book is available from the British Library

On the stroke of midnight, when anything
can happen, Baby Brenda climbs out of her cot,

crawls backwards
down the
$c_re_ak_y$-c_rack_y
stairs,

whizzes across
the kitchen floor,

and ꇘqueezes
through the cat-flap.

The gang is waiting.

Past the slobbering monster that sleeps
in its kennel, they creep.

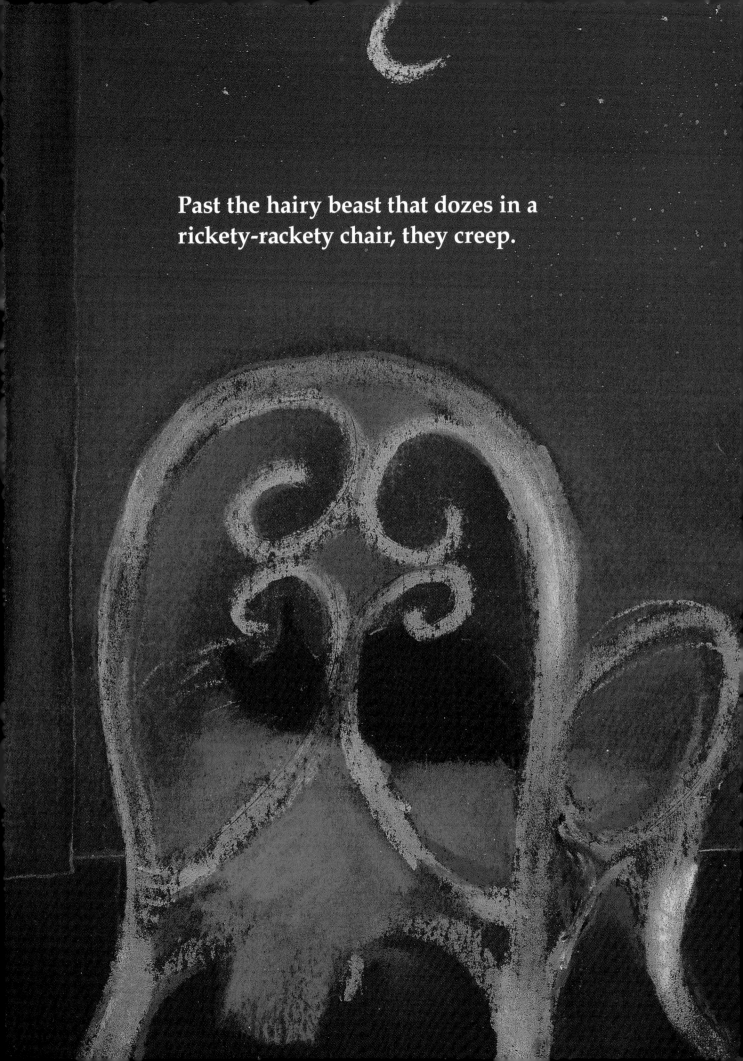

Past the hairy beast that dozes in a rickety-rackety chair, they creep.

Down the driveway
they creep, and out
through the gate.

"Ah," says Baby Brenda
with satisfaction.

Then, quick as quick,
she and her gang toddle
up the road to the park.

Baby Brenda and her gang
do tricky things on the
climbing frame.

Baby Brenda and her gang
whoosh frontwards
(and backwards!)
down the slippery-dip.

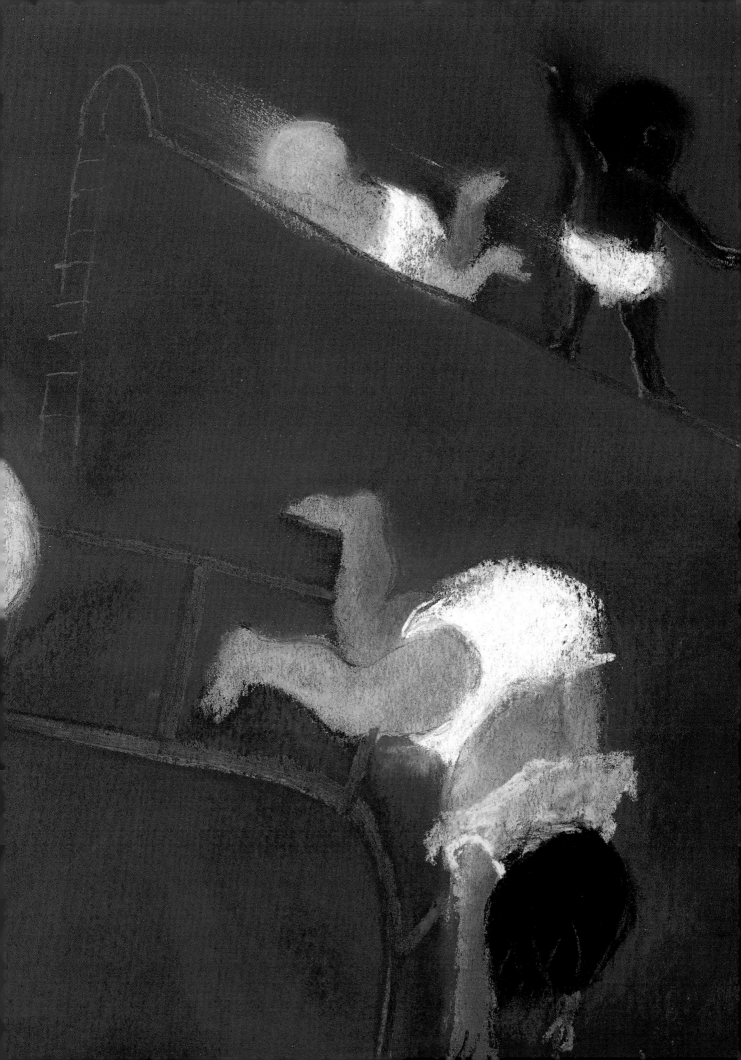

Baby Brenda and her gang
swing on the swings –
up,
down ... up,
down ... up, up, up!

Baby Brenda and her gang swing
high, higher, highest!

They swing so high they hurtle to the moon,

are catapulted onto stars,

and shrieking, shrilling, they cling to
the roller-coaster tail of a comet.

Just as the sun is
coming up, Baby Brenda
and her gang toddle
down the road back home.

In through the gate
and up the driveway,
they creep.

Past the hairy beast lick-licking itself
on the rickety-rackety chair, they creep.

Past the slobbering monster
crunch-crunching on a bone,
they creep.

Baby Brenda says goodbye to her gang.

Then she **SQUEEZES** through the cat-flap,

whizzes across
the kitchen floor,

climbs up the
$c_r e_a k_y$ - $c_r a c k_y$
stairs,

and hops into her cot.

In the morning Baby Brenda's mother puts her in the pram, and takes her and her big sister Vanessa to the park.

"Poor Brenda," says Vanessa. "You're too young

to go on the climbing frame or the slippery-dip.
But if you hold on tight, you can sit on my lap and
have a nice little swing."

"Won't that be exciting!" says Mum.

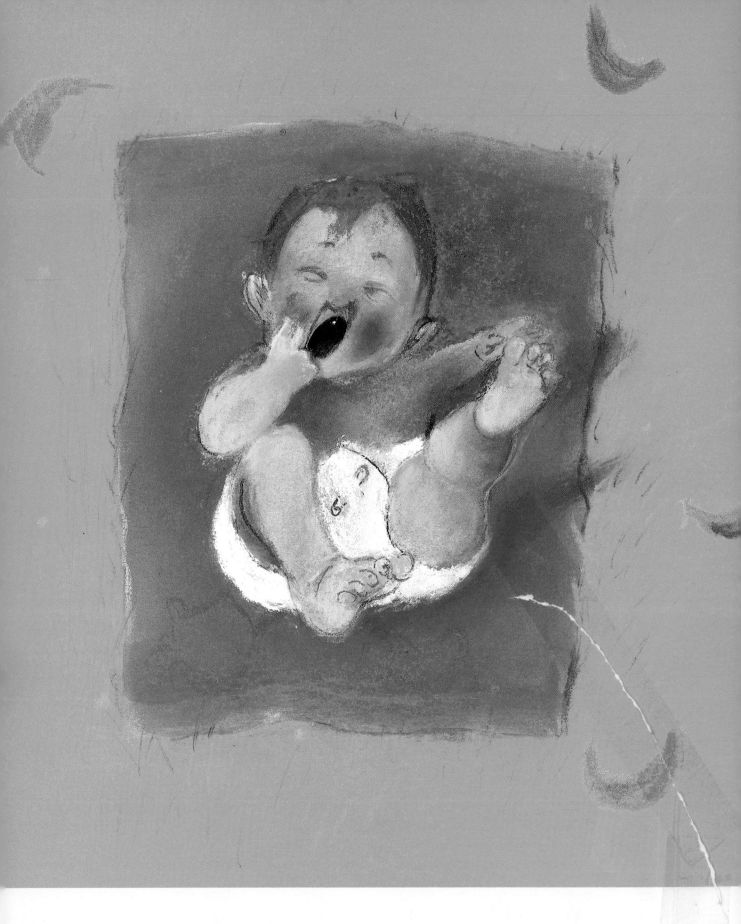

But Baby Brenda just squishes a biscuit
between her fingers, fiddles with her toes,
and *yawn*s.